# BUMBLE B

## Mission ↷ LOST CAT

written by
**Marsha Qualey**

illustrated by
**Jessica Gibson**

LOST CAT
Please Call number below if found

Raintree is an imprint of Capstone Global Library Limited, a company
incorporated in England and Wales having its registered office at 264 Banbury
Road, Oxford, OX2 7DY – Registered company number: 6695582

**www.raintree.co.uk**

**British Library Cataloguing in Publication Data**
A full catalogue record for this book is available from the
British Library.

# CONTENTS

# Meet
# BEATRICE HONEY FLINN
## (aka BUMBLE B.)

# Hi, everyone!

I'm Beatrice Honey Flinn, but I prefer to be called Bumble B. You might think that is a strange name, but it makes a lot of sense. Let me explain:

1 My mum is a beekeeper, and my dad is an artist.

2 I tend to bumble a lot (which is a nice way of saying I'm a little clumsy).

3 My dad says I buzz through life with the persistence and confidence of a bee.

You mix all those reasons with a shortened version of Beatrice, and you get Bumble B. See? It all makes sense.

1 + 2 + 3 =

♥ BUMBLE B.

Mission

LOST
CAT

## Chapter 1

# THE RUNAWAY

Bumble B. waved goodbye
to her mum. She ran along the
pavement to Rosa's house.

Before she rang the bell,
Rosa opened the door. Bumble
B. could see something was
wrong.

"Charley ran away last night!"
Rosa cried. "That curious cat
sneaked out the door when my
mum was bringing in the shopping."

"That's terrible!" said Bumble B.

"I chased after him, but that made him run faster," Rosa said, holding back tears.

"Charley probably thought you were playing a game. Let's go and look for him now," Bumble B. said.

Rosa shook her head. "We've already looked. My dad says we should just wait. He says cats are good at finding their way home."

"I have an idea. Remember how Charley looks out of the window whenever we are in the garden? Maybe if he hears us playing he will come home," Bumble B. said.

"I'll try anything to get Charley back," Rosa said.

They counted extra loud while
they skipped. They jumped and
jumped and jumped.

They rumbled and roared
like dinosaurs as they built a
sandcastle. Then they loudly
stamped it down.

Rosa's younger brother and
sister, Philip and Lucy, joined them
for football.

Everyone shouted as they
played. Still no sign of Charley.

"You were certainly making a lot of noise out there," Rosa's mum said.

"We thought maybe Charley would hear us and come home," Rosa explained.

"Maybe we were too loud," Bumble B. said.

When Bumble B.'s dad came to pick her up, she told him about the missing cat.

"What if we make a flyer? We are going cycling this afternoon. We can put them up around the neighbourhood," he said.

"Yes!" Rosa and her mother said. "That would be great! Thanks so much."

## Chapter 2

# THE FLYER

At home, Bumble B. and her dad got out colouring pens and paper. They sat at the kitchen table.

"Our mission is to find Charley. I know what he looks like, so I will draw the picture. You can do the writing," Bumble B. said.

She drew a picture

of Charley sleeping.

She drew one

of Charley playing

with string.

She drew another one of

him pouncing on Rosa.

"Which drawing is the best?" she asked her dad.

"They are all very nice, but maybe you should show him sitting still," her dad said.

"Good idea!" Bumble B. said. "I will draw him sitting by the window he likes. I bet he is sad now because he misses his family."

Bumble B. drew a few more pictures. Then she and her dad cycled to the library to make photocopies of the flyers.

"Now let's go and hang up these flyers," her dad said.

They got back on their bikes.
It was really windy outside. As
they cycled, a pile of flyers flew
out of Bumble B.'s bike basket.

"Oh no!" she yelled.

"It's okay," her dad said. "We
still have a few we can hand out.
It's better than nothing."

They stopped at a café for a
snack. Bumble B. gave everyone
in the café a flyer. She kept one
to give to Rosa.

On their way home, they rode past Rosa's house.

"We should stop and see if anyone has called about Charley," Bumble B. said.

No one had called.

## Chapter 3

# THE PHONE CALL

Bumble B. wanted to cheer up her friend. She gave Rosa the flyer.

"I lost a lot of them in the wind," Bumble B. said. "But I gave a lot out at the café. Someone will call, I just know it."

"This doesn't look like Charley
at all! You can't even see his stripes
or his white paws," Rosa yelled.
"This is terrible!"

"I wanted to show his face," said Bumble B. "My dad wrote about the stripes and paws in the description."

Rosa threw the flyer down.

"It's a bad drawing, but it doesn't matter. You lost most of the flyers anyway!" Rosa yelled.

Bumble B. felt like crying. She didn't think her drawing was that bad. She was only trying to help.

Rosa's mum rushed in from the kitchen. She waved her phone.

"Someone has found a cat. He is sending a photo," she said.

When Rosa's mum got the photo on her phone, they all looked at it together.

"Charley!" they shouted.

"The man said he was at a café and a young girl with red hair gave him a flyer. When he got home, he spotted a cat in his garden," Rosa's mum said.

"That was me!" Bumble B. said. "We stopped for a snack and I gave flyers to everyone."

"She really did," her dad said. "I had to drag her out of there."

"You are such a good friend, Bumble B.," Rosa's mum said.

Rosa hugged her friend and said, "I am sorry I got angry."

"It's okay," Bumble B. said. "I almost forgot! I have something special for you."

"It's purrfect," Rosa said.

For Rosa and Charley
from Bumble B.

# WRITE ABOUT IT

1. Bumble B. makes flyers for Charley, Rosa's lost cat. Make your own flyer for Charley.

2. Write a letter from Rosa to Bumble B. thanking her for her help.

3. Where do you think Charley went when he left? Pretend you are Charley and write about your adventure.

# TALK ABOUT IT

**1.** Bumble B. feels sad when Rosa tells her that her drawing is bad. Talk about a time when a friend made you feel sad.

**2.** Think about a pet you or a friend owns. If your pet was missing, what would you do?

**3.** If you could have any pet in the world, what would it be? Why?

# GLOSSARY

**bumble**  act or speak in a clumsy way

**café**  small place to eat or get coffee

**description**  use words to explain what something looks like

**flyer**  printed piece of paper that gives information about something

**mission**  special job or task

**pounce**  jump on something suddenly

## ABOUT THE AUTHOR

Marsha Qualey is the author of many books for readers young and old. When she's not writing, she likes to read, go for walks by the river, ski in the winter, garden in the summer and play with her cats all year round. Like Bumble B., she has very good friends who make life fun.

## ABOUT THE ILLUSTRATOR

Jessica Gibson is a freelance illustrator. With a pen and tablet by her side, Jessica loves creating adorable, whimsical and quirky illustrations, ready to brighten everyone's hearts.

# FUN
## Doesn't stop here!

You can read more books about Bumble B. and her friends.

## Discover more at
## WWW.RAINTREE.CO.UK